Sociopaths Buy Better Flowers

A short story collection
by
Addison N. James

Sociopaths Buy Better Flowers

Copyright Steven Cagnina
All Rights Reserved.

Sociopaths Buy Better Flowers

To J,S,N, and M.

I am in thanks forever to all of you

Sociopaths Buy Better Flowers

CONTENTS

War
A long love scene, a short hallway
Call Me... Frank
The Three Relationships of Eve
Cruel and Unjust in the Afternoon
The Hot Black Night

WAR

The ocean had a summer sun landing on it in the distance that pinched up a watery orange horizon. Nick stood at the edge of the waves, watching little white froths boil into the sand as the water retreated. There was nothing like a beach breeze to close your eyes to and a slight smile crossed over Nick's face as he heard the sea gulls fly and almost land. But then his eyes opened and his peripheral vison caught a tall slim figure, dressed down in a perfect power grey suit and solid blue tie, hair thick, slick and unmoving against the breeze.

"Hello Tom."

"Well, hello Nick. "

Nick closed his eyes again and shrugged. "So what's wrong with Sylvia?" he said. He thought, I hate this fucker.

****

The small bar, decorated with outdated football schedules and random stuffed fish, had a white trash neon glow in the late afternoon; it was quiet and unfilled, its middle-aged bartender a little plump and a whole lot sassy. Her name was Carol and her eyes drifted up suspiciously as she put the pitcher nearer to Nick than Tom. "On your usual bill honey," she said. "Or should I give it to Mr. Fancy here?"

Tom looked away, noticeably trying to hide his arrogant disdain. "It's got charm, Nick. A good place for a movie scene."

Nick smirked. He was always fascinated how agents were writing movie scenes. They were the last people nature should have given language abilities. "What's wrong with Sylvia?" Nick repeated. He didn't think it'd be necessary to bluntly tell Tom to fuck off. But he would soon if the bastard didn't get to the point.

"She's 35," Tom said.

"Yes. That does sound tragic."

"You didn't let me finish. She's 35 but looks 25 and the offers are still rolling in for parts in their late 20's. Romantic comedies. Dramas. Anything."

"Wonderful."

Tom nodded woefully. He took a sip. "I know you hate it but she loves it. Or she used to. She says she's done, Nick. Quit. She's quit the business. Since her mother died last year, she's been inconsolable and all over the place. And she left Henry a few months ago."

"Maybe she's just free now."

"Nick, I am not gonna sit here and turn on the bullshit agent charm. Which we both know you'd hate."

"Funny Tom, but this sounds like bullshit agent charm to me. Agents are always pretending they're not what surrounds them. They're not the fancy parties and that ridiculous suit and any other bullshit. But that's all you are, so fucking tell me what you want from me."

Tom nipped at his cheap beer. At least it was cold. "Nothing except to go down there to her favorite place in the world and check on her. She's thrown out her phone, none of her entourage is with her and even Ray her bodyguard has been cut off. I want you to go down there, all expenses paid." He reached in his wallet and took out a black, heavy credit card with Nick's name on it. "I want you to go down there and just see how she is."

"No you don't. You want me to talk her back."

"Nick – you'd be the last person to do that. Come on! You know that. But you're the only person real to her anymore, I think."

"No," Nick said, and for a second all the past pain made the no seem definitive. But Tom didn't get to be the agent he was by not reading people and closing. Nick's no came from another place than his green eyes were, and Tom could see only Sylvia in them.

"All I want, Nick, is for you to go down there and make sure she's ok. Send me one text that says situation not fatal and that's it. I had you booked into an open ended trip. You can stay down there as long as you want – everything inside the hotel is paid for and this credit card pays for anything else. She's hurting, Nick. This isn't about me. Or you. You know how much she loved her mother. It was complicated and now she's gone and Sylvia is all alone. Go down there, give her a hug. That's it. Please?"

Nick looked over at his bartender, who was openly eavesdropping. Her dark eyes shot a no at him, so he looked away. He'd tried for a long time to not look ahead, but that was what he was going to have to do now. "Make sure I have a black non-descript car waiting for me," he said.

****

Twilight really was the best time and this black slim car was perfect. Sylvia, a white shirt wrapped around her waist, a blue tank-top and jean shorts fashionably tight, tapped her beige sandals toward a red scooter. Her dark hair was as long and lovely as he remembered, and her thin, tight frame had nothing superfluous on it and seemed to live to stretch her small breasts upward. Her oversized shades covered the dark brown eyes which had stared into him on many walks.

    Sylvia took off her sunglasses and away she went.

"Where are you going, baby?" Nick whispered and calmly turned the engine over and followed.

The house was so rundown it had become more of a shack; inside rested Reesce, a very old islander whose dark skin seemed to be on its third layer of wrinkles. A long time ago Sylvia and Nick had sat drinking rum all night while this kind and salty bartender, straight out of central casting, served them. He even let them stay after close and Sylvia paid a helluva tip to him. There was a kindness to him that Sylvia found irresistible. He seemed to look at her with father's eyes she always wished for—in her world, father's eyes had love but not a lot of connection and mother's eyes had disapproval and expectations and impossible needs. Nick knew that after any personal setbacks, romantic or career wise, she traveled down here and spent all night in Reesce's bar, drinking and tipping him insanely. But he had cancer now. Her mother died from cancer. She already had several cancer scares herself and it seemed to Sylvia after her mother died, everyone had cancer. Nick understood. He'd lost a brother to it. Nothing cuts off possibilities like losing someone you love. You don't just see their end – you see *the end*. Cancer was a ubiquitous reminder that you're just passing through and no one has all the time in the world.

Sylvia pulled up to Reesce's sad home; outside stood an official looking man – he had an arrogant, professional stance that cried doctor. Sylvia reached into her back pocket and pulled out a check. The doctor man smiled for a moment and Nick could see his smile sickened Sylvia. He could see it, too, and he quickly put on his grave face. Sylvia then turned on her movie-star smile and they both went into see Reesce.

****

It took about an hour for the doctor and Sylvia to exit and when Sylvia saw Nick sitting on her scooter as if he owned it, a smile took over her that wasn't exactly full of surprise. There was something unmatched, something that couldn't be taken away or, frustratingly – added to, between them. When everything else failed, it still survived. It was always just a phone call away. In a maudlin, drunken moment, Nick had once told her that life might be worth living if it was always just one touch away, and that night she cried a little. She never told him, though.

Sylvia quickly dismissed the doctor and then ran to hug Nick. Her thin warmth fell into him and it was easy to remember how holding her was such a narcotic. "How?" she said.

"You have such a kind and caring agent."

"No!"

"He was willing to pay. I extracted both kidneys. Strange, but did you know agents are born with three kidneys? It must be the need to piss away so many lives."

Sylvia hugged him again. "Where are you staying?"

"Baby, you know where."

Sylvia's smile got more heightened. "Let's go out! I'm sooooo glad to see you! Let's get back –" She frowned at her scooter. "I can't fit two on this thing!"

Nick slowly got off the scooter. "Baby what did you think I did? Walk? See that car right there? I stole it. We got mid-ranged priced, fuel economic wheels."

Sylvia laughed. And then she hugged Nick again.

****

"For an island, they certainly do have great steak," Nick said.

Sylvia dug into her salmon. "Yes they do. And this salmon is awesome. I cannot believe you're here."

"You'll believe it when I start to wear your underwear. I packed light. What was going on in that house anyway?"

"It's Reesce. When I got here, I went to our favorite little bar. He wasn't there – and you know he always worked 24/7. The help there told me what happened to him. Cancer." Her voice broke at the sound of that word. "Anyway, I just wanted to help him. I am really glad to see you, Nick."

"Me too, baby. Me too. You're such a kind person. I am glad you did what you could for Reesce." Nick knew

Sylvia had paid that "doctor" not to treat him, but to drug him. People Reesce's age don't fight it. Heavy drugs are their only salvation.

The waiter brought over a second bottle of pinot noir. "Is this really really really expensive?" Nick asked.

The waiter nodded.

"Good. Because I'd hate Tom's kids to get into too good of a college. When this one's done, bring another."

As the waiter exited, Sylvia and Nick drifted back into good times past. It was their ritual. Always amazement at actually being in each other's presence, followed by remember-when talk, and then, as the wine soaked in and the moon rose higher, deeper waters. One thing in Sylvia as sure as her blood and natural beauty was a positive outlook. For many years, Nick had suspected it to be fake, but as they went from teenagers to twenty-somethings, he realized that fake or real was never a proper distinction. No, her propensity to twist things into best-of scenarios was just there, as much as her brown eyes and delicate mouth. Type-A achievers have something that the rest can't grasp: the ability to process horrors without dwelling on them. They just put the best spin on them and move on while the rest of us are anchored to our failures and losses. It took him years to understand that Sylvia calling him in the middle of the night in the throes of self-doubt about her marriage or career didn't mean that the next day, she'd be torn in the direction of that self-doubt. If she doubted she could pull off a role, she'd cry to Nick over a long call, resolve to maybe find something else, something she really wanted, maybe even leave the business, and always end the call by telling him she loved him. And then the next day, a new resolve had grown seemingly in her sleep, and suddenly this role was what *she had to do*. It was right and great and belatedly, she'd tell Nick she was going ahead with it, but she loved him.

This same pattern was repeated when it came to relationships. Oh the doubts she had with Henry! The late-night phone calls that made Nick think she was going to call it off. But then one day, he got a text. Not a call, not even an email; a text that said: I'm engaged. Can you believe it?...

But Nick was here to see if the achiever-resolve had failed to grow this time around. He'd been an underachiever. He wrote one successful movie, mostly thanks to Sylvia's connections, then pissed away all other opportunities. Luckily, he'd make a good investment or two and, far from rich – he could never have afforded this trip, he'd settled into a life of early oceanic middle-age. He never quit writing. He just quit trying to pretend he was a writer. Now he did the odd bartending gig here and there and mostly slept alone. His dreams weren't full of Sylvia because why sleep in that kind of pain?

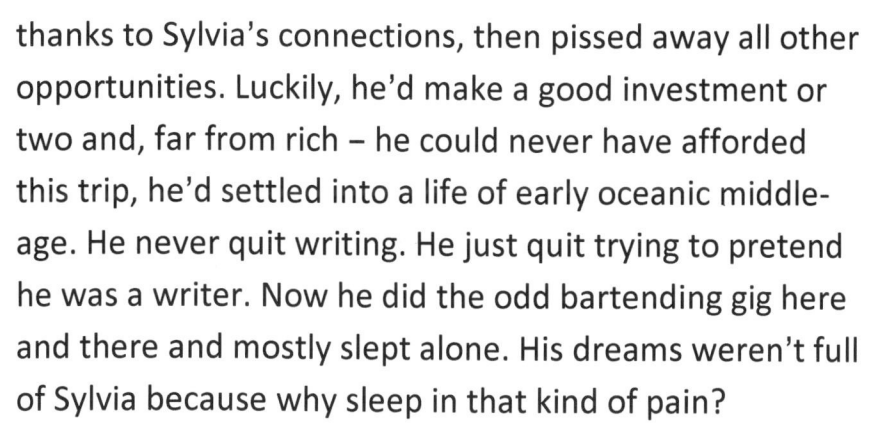

Nick was sure that Sylvia lived in perpetual doubt. She had been living a life of success to make up for her mother's failures and that pride in her mother's eyes was enough to get her by, but not enough to convince her that the life she had was really hers. Mother-daughter relationships are never easy for anyone, but theirs was one that made Sylvia grow up fast, often feeling as the parent even as her mother whipped her along to keep focused, to marry well, to never give in to tough-luck cases. When you are as pretty and famous as Sylvia, it's very easy to find a rich man who is also kind. But what was between Nick and Sylvia, something born from his teenage lust into an insurmountable loyalty and empathy, you cannot choose on a menu. But when the guy was Nick and seemed to find defeat even in success'

bosom, you didn't say I do. You said, I love you, and remember when?

Another bottle of wine was now finished and Sylvia's dark, brown eyes suddenly watered. "Nick," she said, "I just can't take it anymore. I miss mom so much."

Nick reached over and touched her hand. Its tremble made him think that, maybe for the first time in her life, Sylvia was broken. Broken like the rest of us, he thought. Not a movie-star now, not a beautiful woman charmed with achievement. Just a girl who had lost her mother, lost her signpost. Lost the reasons why she was what she was. Nick had never loved her more but he also felt a sinking unease. Something suddenly felt finalized, but he had no idea what that something was. Keep drinking Nick, he thought, and don't mention it.

****

"So how rich is Henry anyway? Perfume empire, right?"

"Very," Sylvia laughed. And then she picked up the phone. "Two bottles of – what were we drinking at dinner? – who cares. Bring us expensive pinot noir.

"Me either. Sometimes I think: Nick, why didn't you just play the game? Sylvia had it setup for you. Why did you fuck up so much?"

"I hate all the bullshit. Henry's functions. His business charities and then mine and parties and blah blah. And I can't tell anyone. People are starving and I'm complaining about being an actress!"

"Well, in the Twitter-world, no you can't. Publicly. But you know, I've learned there is no degree of worth to living. Rich, poor. You deal with the consequences of the life in front of you. Yes, it seems trivial that a rich actress doesn't want to lead that life, that black-tie parties are too much for her! But then, all you have is the heart and brain and soul you have and the life you lead. You can't just not answer your own existential questions because people are starving in Africa."

Sylvia poured them both fresh glasses. "You always have a way of making me feel understood. How are you, anyway? I really want to know."

He believed her. But no way he was going to answer. "I'm me," he said. "So you threw away your phone, left Henry and fired Tom."

"Tom obviously doesn't believe he's fired. He wants me to star in this war drama. I'd play an Italian mom that loses her husband, who was a coward and avoided War World One but dies anyway when their village gets attacked, and then am forced to save her family through a series of hellish adventures until I reach the American saviors at the end. He says the studio is treating it as a December drama and the role would be really wrenching from a physical point of view as I fight for my children. He sees Oscar."

Sylvia's voice had gotten a tad higher as she explained the pitch, and her eyes even turned on a bit. This made Nick a little sad. Just a little because it wasn't entirely unexpected. "So why don't you take it? Go out on a high note?"

"Silly," she said. "I told you. I'm done. Now all I want is –"

"All you want is what?" Nick said, a terse edge in his voice.

"To be left alone. To have time for this."

Nick smiled. "Let's sit on that soft bed again," he said.

****

"It's really comfortable," Sylvia said as she stretched sideways on the bed before him. There was nothing sexier than a woman lying on her side as she tried to seduce you. Nick looked at the clock. It was 3am. "The dark night of the soul time," he said.

"What?"

"Fitzgerald. He wrote that. In the dark night of the soul, it is always 3am. Well it's 3am now. Isn't it?"

Sylvia inched one of her legs closer to his. "It's late enough," she said.

It was at this moment that Nick did what he always did. He plucked failure from a full success of apple-trees. He leaned over and kissed Sylvia's cheek. "At twilight tomorrow, I am gonna knock on your door. You better be here, baby." And before she could protest, he was gone. She tipped her body flat on the bed as Nick slammed the door; everything suddenly felt flat and defeated and her eyes last sight before slumber was the white ceiling fan breaking down – it was barely turning. She could relate.

****

Sylvia woke early. Her first thoughts were of Nick and his refusal to just give in to the moment. She had often refused the natural fruit of such a moment with him, but this time, throwing herself in front of him – clearly in need, and he didn't bite. Why? It was easy and quick to blame his heart as one of a coward, but Sylvia's mind wasn't so artless. No, now over breakfast and the breaking morning she felt as much responsible for Nick leaving last night as he was. She had managed to spend two decades pushing him away as much as embracing him, and on those rare occasions that their mouths had connected, she'd stopped short of going all the way. And she was aware how crippling imagination and hope were when they decided to get together. What if it all turned out wrong – how crushing would that be to lose both the hope that one day your soul mate would find you and your imagination's power to create that oasis in your mind? Could she handle calling Nick an ex-anything? Could he handle calling her an ex-anything? Can you know somebody so well that you're a liability in their daily lives?

    Sylvia wondered about this and the past and the future as the daylight stubbornly stood in the sky. She wondered about what Nick was wondering about. And then twilight, the magic hour, came and Nick, always on time, knocked at her door. She smiled and opened the door and then told him to count to twenty before entering.

Nick counted to twenty. He even closed his eyes, even though he was not told to do so. And then he walked inside the suite, closing the door as delicately as he could. As he was turning toward the bedroom, Sylvia stood before him, naked, smiling and yet, scared, her clothes in patches behind her.

    Nick looked at her – looked from top to bottom at her faultless skin and trembling curves – and the raw sexual desire for her he'd killed off years ago instantly lit again. The air was pure electricity as Nick leaned in for a kiss, a kiss that turned passionate and slow and then he pulled back his lips into a smile. "Although I respect such a bold fashion choice, I'm not sure the hotel restaurant has such a David Bowie type of aesthetic."

    He smiled at Sylvia's instant confusion and fear. He gave her another kiss and then picked up her blue panties. "You see they may want these, for health code reasons. Damn liberal legislation." He moved his hand slowly, very slowly, along the inner thigh of both of Sylvia's legs; he reached into her eventually and she shook and her legs came apart and then he slid his thumb gently around her center – he kept up the pressure for a gentle while until finally moving his hand down her right leg; he lifted the leg into her underwear, and then did so with her left side, gingerly pulling the cloth upward until she was covered. "Yes. They might want these."

    Now Nick picked up her red bra and began kissing at her navel, moving slowly with baby kisses over her stomach until he reached her nipples, staying engaged on both for a while and then, rising, he took her into his arms and placed her bra over her, pulling her toward him as he strapped it closed. Then he looked into her dark brown eyes and said, "Let's skip that top down there." He went to her closet and came out with a blue silk top that sat as light as a feather over her. He then picked Sylvia up and gently placed her on the soft bed. Going between her thighs for a moment, he put a pair of jeans over her while never breaking eye contact.

"You could try to go barefoot, but I'd stick with those sandals just to be safe," he said. He grabbed her hand, pulling her toward him. "Did I ever tell you I might love you?" he said. And with a smile, Nick then guided Sylvia out the door, toward the yellow glow of the hallway's lamps.

****

Sylvia looked at Nick with new eyes. She was almost breathless at his confidence. He meticulously ordered the appetizers and wine and he even ordered the entrees for both of them. By reversing the usual process of sex he had somehow extended the foreplay. It was exciting seeing a man so willing to wait and yet, keep engaged enough with his eyes and wordplay that she knew all he was thinking of was getting her back to the bedroom he had boldly, bravely, and not a little bit stupidly, walked out of twice. But this last time was the ultimate message she felt any woman would want to hear: You're worth the wait – he was buying her dinner first, even though he didn't have to, because that was how much he loved her. She was more than sex, but thanks to that glint in his eyes, she knew she was also totally sex to him as well.

    Nick called for the check after the second bottle of wine and they walked silently to the elevator and then to her room. Between them was a warm anticipation. As they got closer to her room, their hands enveloped, and then Sylvia pulled out her key. After she had opened the door, she turned and attacked Nick and he didn't retreat. In seconds she was on that soft bed, naked, held, kissed, penetrated, loved, and known. In all the chaos that sex creates, not once was there any doubt between them, and when Sylvia fell asleep after talking about her mom, it was a deep sleep. In fact, she'd never understand what made her wake up before dawn and do what she did.

****

Nick awoke and, seeing Sylvia gone, smiled. He wondered what she was up to – ordering wine? Taking a moonlight walk? Investigating, he got up and saw a light coming through the half-open bedroom door. Stepping into the main room, he saw Sylvia in the corner, staring at the glowing screen of a large, expensive phone. She shook when she noticed him. She almost spoke – she almost lied, but then all the history between them forced a deeper respect. "I was just checking it," she finally said.

    Nick felt punched. It all hit him in an instant. "We sleep together and then you check the phone you claim to not have anymore? Am I to believe there is no correlation?"

    Sylvia threw the phone down and approached him. "No no no no!" she said. "There isn't. It's –"

    "Bullshit!"

    "No!"

"Just working out your doubts, huh? Taking a look at the other side, until you decide to go with the status quo – which you always fucking do. Fuck you, Sylvia!"

"Nick it isn't *this*!"

"Isn't it!"

"Since mom died, it's just been so hard."

"Well my brother died. Cancer."

Sylvia was taken aback. "What? Why didn't you tell me?"

Nick smirked. "Because I deluded myself that I was helping you. My brother is dead, he's gone and all this seems like just…pointless and old and I don't why we bother. I really don't." He suddenly felt out of breath and sat down on the couch. He put a hand up to tell her to stop her approach. He'd always had a talent for identifying patterns, for seeing connections – and this inexplicable talent suddenly shouted an answer at him. "Fucking Tom is brilliant, isn't he?"

Sylvia, half-naked from the bottom down, felt breathless herself as the moonlight trickled in from the badly drawn shade over the balcony doors. "What do you mean?"

"Well, *my love*. Tom knows you'll be back. Eventually. But this picture has a deadline and his stall time is reaching an end. He knows it's a hit. So he sends me to you. You know, to 'check on you.' All innocent. But what he knows is that the vulnerable you will embrace me and then do what you always do: retreat. Right back to the life. To him. Just in time for the movie! Fucker played me. He's even more of a prick than I thought he was, but he's a lot smarter than I considered."

Sylvia did a few stops and starts, protests and even, when they failed, accusations. But they didn't work because she didn't believe in any of them.

Nick got off the couch, grabbed Sylvia – and there was nothing gentle about his touch this time. "Don't you see! *You're* the type of person that can only be understood by her *agent*! Not even I, after all these years, understand you as much as that prick!"

"Nick you're being unfair. Who the fuck are you to judge me?"

"The guy who just slept with you thinking you meant what you said. That's who I am. But that's not who you are. You're a movie-star, baby. You're a *success*!

And I am sick of being your vacation. You're going back to that perfume-prick. You're going back to Hollywood. Which is all fine except that it isn't you – except for the first time – the *first* time in all these years, I realize it *is* you. Well I'm tired of being me and you being you."

Nick noticed Sylvia's body was now shivering and her beautiful face had become grotesque from despair. This was one of those moments. He could turn this upward – like she would – he could make the best of it. Or he could kill. But if this was all about her ultimately being what she was, then it was also about him being what he ultimately was. "You're nothing but a collection of trophies," he said. He instantly knew there were kinder words and embraces he'd killed forever by saying that. He'd murdered everything. And he did so even as he loved her more than ever. In brief, intense spurts, she could be his, but now, in the bloody aftermath of all their unspoken selves coming forward as the truth, he couldn't rely on the old narrative for comfort. It was usually his failure and cowardice that kept them apart.

But now, maybe it was hers – and that killed all hope in him.

He didn't kiss Sylvia goodbye as he left. He didn't even close the front door. He just walked with eyes down, each step faster than the last.

****

Perhaps it was out of sadism, or maybe just hurting helped him to know he wasn't all the way dead yet, but Nick did attend the opening weekend of Sylvia's new war picture. The reviews were raves and the audience was with Sylvia's plucky character every step of the way. Outside the theater, the dark blue of tropical December skies hung over the people as they walked and shopped and said *Tis 'the season*. But here in the dim light, a movie played to triumphant applause and it was all too much. As the audience clapped over the credits, Nick got up fast and left through the emergency exit doors, leaving behind Sylvia's deadening applause, he hoped, forever.

A long love scene, a short hallway

He didn't care what bipolar madness had brought her here. Sure, she was vulnerable, but she was here now. A lot worse for wear, 24 and no longer boring because she was here.

"May I have some wine or a beer?" she asked.

He stood at the end of his long living room, staring her down from top to bottom, her long blonde hair just a few shades less than combed, her messy green eyes watery. But there was no denying that she was beautiful when you took her all in - her downward, gun-shy eyes, hair that was elegant even when messy, the shapely tight body boxed in perfectly by the tight blue jeans - all of her was full and alive. He had held her briefly before, kissed her even more briefly, but unlike her, he was much older and knew the true value of what she had: Beautiful youth. But it was mixed up in a crazy, sad mind that hadn't figured out her own freakishness yet. It wasn't as if he was without his own mental disturbances, but hers was just like her beauty and potential – fresh and unexamined.

"No, you cannot have anything to drink," he said, and then he smiled. He walked toward his computer, flicked at a few buttons and suddenly the room was awash in gentle guitar strumming and dreaming lyrics. Before she could blink her watery eyes, he was holding her, his hands aggressively moving over her back, ripping up her tucked-in blousy shirt. Tighter and tighter she closed against him, her hands and lips at first reticent. Always with a 24 year-old girl there is doubt about sleeping with someone who might actually understand her, but eventually the strength of his grip felt safe and she fell against his broad shoulders. And then suddenly it was she who was kissing him aggressively, tearing at his jeans and loose shirt.

The warmth of her bare skin against his felt like peace, and for a moment he stopped his tearing-eroticism – against the harmonies they improvised a close dance and her heart steadied as his took off. Looking at her sad eyes again, he pushed her messy but lovely hair back and then kissed her with a gentle ferociousness that was completely new for her. Boys her own age were usually aggressive, and they could be animals – but none had showed the slowing down gentleness that he was now – it occurred to her that what she thought had been passion and desire really was just awkward, thoughtless hormones.

He sensed that for now, she didn't really want much foreplay. So it was quick after he placed her on his bed and removed her panties that he was inside of her. But the penetration was not quick. It was at times fast, slow, measured, and filled with grappling hands, but it was never quick and the longer he stayed inside of her, the more she felt she had made the right decision to seek him out tonight.

Lying side by side in the darkness, he laughed now. "Now you can have that drink."

She smiled and rolled against him so her small breasts heated his side. "Tonight some shit went down," she said.

"Don't tell me." He paused. "At least yet."

The good thing about bipolar disorder is it doesn't lack for words. Or transient thoughts. She had plenty to say. "I was thinking about that thing you told me. About what happens after you choose someone to write about. By the way, are you planning to write about me?"

"No," he lied. But it was a lie more to himself than her.

"Rearview mirrors," she said.

"When you choose to write about someone you irretrievably put them in the rearview mirror of your life. It's fucking true."

"Is it? I mean, I've been writing songs about this guy for a while and he seems very *present* to me. You know what I'm saying?"

"You're not writing honestly about him. You're just writing him to stay close to him. Writing is backwards, the past. If you wrote about him honestly, you'd see what a shit he is, because the only reason someone like you would write and obsess about someone is if they had a knack for wounding you. Such is the state of being a lonely 24 year old in a giant fucked-up whatever this is."

He looked at her now, his eyes high and sideways down on her confused face.

"I don't like the way you talk down to me," she whispered.

"I'm the only one in your fucking life that doesn't talk down to you. You get a little older and everything is shorter. Time is shortest. You don't have that much time and wasting it on one night stands and irrational decisions that you can blame on being crazy isn't healthy. It'll give you a tragic country love song or two. But it's easy to be crazy. Crazy is all surface. I know. I'm crazier than you, my dear. I just learned it isn't all that interesting."

She got up, her naked frame slight against the moonlight coming through the thin curtains. It was easy to see her now as some portrait a great painter would have created, a delicate beautiful sexual creature standing against a romantic moon – but somehow even in the indistinct darkness you still knew how sad she was. He'd never let her know, but he wanted to get up and somehow make this sadness physical so he could rip it out of her, heal her. He had that same unknowable sadness and it would be glorious to know that at least someone could be cured of it.

She paced in little strides as she asked, "Do you think people like us are hopeless?"

"I'm a writer. A failed one, but nevertheless a good one. Really good. Everyone is hopeless."

"No, don't give me bullshit philosophy! Are people like me and you really *hopeless*?"

"You mean writers with mental handicaps? I think what you're asking me is after all the bullshit are we just too crazy to be loved. I am better than a decade older than you. And tonight I was alone when you knocked on the door. And you knocked on that door because you knew I'd be alone. Does that answer your question?"

"Every time I love anyone I obsess over things and it all just fills up. Like water on a sinking boat. Claustrophobic. And noisy." She smiled. "Claustrophobic and noisy. I am gonna use that as a song title!"

"What is it you want?"

"To be a successful songwriter."

"You said that *quick*, didn't you?"

"What do you mean?"

"You didn't say happy. Or loved. You said successful at being creative." He got up suddenly, wrapping her into his arms in an instant. "You may be 24. You may be doomed. But that was the honest answer of a real artist." She could feel him rise against her. "I've never wanted anyone more than I do you right now," he said, and before she could blink she was thrown on the bed and he was on top of her. But unlike last time, as he moved inside of her, she wondered if coming here was a good idea after all. His moving against her didn't feel close and secure. It felt like an invasion.

The kitchen was lit only by the open refrigerator door. She opened a beer and handed it to him and then opened one for herself.

"You know, in bed just now, I felt invaded by you somehow. Like you were taking stuff from me that wasn't on sale."

He smiled at her phrasing. Songwriters, novel writers, poets – they can't help but compose when others would just speak. "Was it a planned invasion and if so, who planned it? You or I?"

She smiled. "That's a good question, isn't it?"

"A very good fucking question," he said.

They stood in silence for a moment. "I told you on our first drinking night that hurting people isn't sexy or complicated or dangerous. It's just cruel. I did more than my share of cruelty at your age and beyond. I have no desire to hurt you. Taking things is just part of life."

She thought about that for a moment and then her fast mind wandered into, "Somehow this kitchen is even smaller when it's dark." But neither of them moved from it.

"Tell me what sordid humiliating thing happened tonight," he said.

"I keyed his car. I mean, I *really* keyed his car. I might get arrested."

"What was his crime?"

"I fucked him last night even though I knew he had a girlfriend. Tonight I walked into a bar and saw him with her."

He took a big sip. "Doesn't sound like much of a villain, does he? A piece of shit boyfriend, sure. But not much more mystery than that is there? But oh so many words you've heartbreakingly sung about him!"

"Everything just got so fast and I just couldn't imagine living, going on unless I *did* something about this right now, right now and so I did, I went outside, took out my big house key and went to town on his fucking red sports car, fucking jackass, and then I just felt out of my body, myself and like something bigger and electric had taken control of me and was pushing me ahead like some kind of fucked train."

"And how many times this week have you felt that way?"

She laughed. "Probably twenty. You feel it, too, don't you?"

"All the time."

"How do you keep from acting it out?"

He took a few sips as he thought about his answer. He really wanted to answer this honestly. "I don't always. Some of it is age and mellowing. A lot of writers are depressives, bipolars, and all kinds of science goes on to figure out why. Maybe it's as easy as this: Crazy people need drama – we're drama queens. And drama and conflict tell the best stories. I don't know why I don't go out and bust up women's apartments anymore because they dared hurt me. It helps to date very few women." He looked around the small kitchen and then gestured to it. "Helps to admit you're consigned to a very small space, I guess. And it's a lonely lonely space, isn't it?" He said the last line in a mocking tone that, rather than protect him, actually exposed him more to her.

She finished her beer and took out another one, the brief light of the fridge unsettling him for a moment. "Why did I come here tonight?"

"I find it boring answering for you. You explain it to me."

"But you know why."

"Who fucking cares what I know."

"I feel cold all of a sudden. Will you hold me?"

"No," he said and closed the small space between them. He took the cold, full beer out of her hand. "But I will fuck you again." His hands moved over her tight ass and then her stomach. He lowered his face until her back arched and her legs jailed him, and they both closed their eyes tighter. The small space and the total darkness were suddenly heaven as the blood rushed high and neither noticed all the kitchen appliances breaking on the floor.

An unsexy consequence of oral sex is after it's done, a practical bathroom break is needed. She could hear the rapid scrapes of his toothbrush and then the medicinary splash of mouthwash hitting the sink. What am I doing here? she thought. Why am I so afraid of him?

Expecting to have another long talk as he climbed into bed, instead they both welcomed silence as it came between them. He was much wiser than she was, but wisdom is not intelligence and she was plenty smart. And talented. He heard her music and she was good and that made her even more irresistible to him. He knew the universe was tipped her way to be successful if she could just stop worshiping and mystifying her illness. No, he was made of concrete, he was sure, but she was still soft clay, able and maybe even had a surprise or two in her. But his heart began to race because he was sure she wouldn't surprise him tonight and why the hell did he let her in, anyway? He could lie the great male lie and tell himself it was for the sex but that's not what this was. Sure, he was lonely, but he was even lonelier lying against her thin, warm frame now because he knew this lovely thing had nowhere to go but out that door. The moon was only going to shine through those weak curtains for so long.

"I'm a phony, you know," he said. "I talk down to you, tell you how to be a good bipolar but I'm no better off even at my age. I let you in because I'm a freak like you're a freak. We're a little off – just away from the rest of the world. Normal people, non-writers, etc – they have the same shitty problems we do but these people wake up every day and are afraid of terrorism or cancer or whatever. You know what people like us fear? *Ourselves.* We know we're the first line of destruction for our lives. I let you in tonight because I was lonely and I knew you were just scared enough of your life to let me take you for a while."

"Every time we drink together in that crappy bar, I feel good because you understand me. And we're both word people. We just talk and talk and talk. Bipolars with wordy needs. It's nice to talk to someone who understands."

"But it isn't nice to fuck them. Especially when they're older."

"I didn't say that."

"Oh yes you did." He smiled cruelly. "The truth is that I could make you happy and you don't want to be happy. The truth is I'm a selfish bastard who in the end would lose you anyway even if I made you happy. The truth is you deserve your 24 year-old doubt, and I find it boring. 24 and boring. 44 and lost. Aren't we the kind of couple who eats out on Saturday nights?"

He got up from the bed and sat at his desk chair. "I think you should leave and never come back."

"You're a shit, you know that? You're just trying to win the breakup. You think I am gonna leave when the sun comes out and never come back."

"Aren't you?"

"Yes!"

"And what does that tell you?"

"It scares the shit out of me because what if in twenty years I am still like you and anyone that could feel for me runs away?"

"Or you try to win the breakup?" He laughed. "I feel the need to tell you the absolute horrible-est truth right now. I know you're going to leave. I know I am gonna feel bad. I knew you'll be a story that just isn't enough down the road. And I really wanna fuck you one last time anyway."

She got up from the bed and coldly put on her clothes. Sending the freeze his way felt like the right thing to do, but once her sandals were on, something pulled her toward him.

She just couldn't leave without gently kissing him goodbye and so she did.

He said nothing. Nothing new was explained tonight, nothing was found to enlighten. Her exit just re-enforced his known fate. But he kissed her gently back and hoped that maybe something tonight might change for her, that maybe something in the future wouldn't be so afraid and she'd take a chance, mix up the puzzle, give in to that which has little drama but so much erotic mystery. That maybe she'd allow herself to be more than an artist - to be kind. Maybe she'll be alright, he thought, as she closed the front door and walked the short hallway to the aged elevator outside. It was a short walk to get on it and then go down, down, down. But maybe she'll be alright. If I were kinder, which I'm not, I'd even write it down that way. But I'm not kind, he thought. I'm alone.

Call Me...Frank

Her murderer moved through the apartment as if he lived there. But he'd never been there before tonight, although he'd imagined it many times. And it amused him how the couches were blue and the television was black and both were aligned to reduce the glare of sunlight through the balcony drapes. This is exactly how his apartment was setup, and he stopped at the fridge to see if it contained the same tomato juice he loved, the same organic brown eggs he insisted on, and the same orange juice containers which had been repurposed into tap water holders. Sure enough, all of these things were there, and a smile crossed his mis-shaven face. His green eyes twinkled. He had always been a jerk about being right, and this was the coolest thing he had ever been right about. Except he couldn't tell anybody. Except Elizabeth, but she was about to die. Rising from the two day old sheets on her bed, she called out, "Frank."

He dropped his blue computer bag and took out the

ropes. Into the doorway he appeared, lifeless for a moment in black jeans and a blank white t-shirt, his twinkled eyes receding into focus. His poorly shaved face poked out a few stray grey hairs down his neck. "You look beautiful," he said. And he thought it was odd how sincerely he meant that.

Elizabeth hated the stiffness of this bedroom. It was hot, no matter how much she ran the AC, and there were always books and computer cables and movies on the floor, a white rug aged into an unflattering pale brown holding it all up. The rug always needed vacuuming, and what it really needed was to be gone, replaced like the bed and the drapes and the bad housekeeping habits of Frank with something fresh and clean. I married the wrong man, she occasionally considered, but that always passed quickly, and she mostly clung to Frank's kindness. She connected with him. He wasn't a naturally cruel person, more of a sensitive artist-type. For a woman who was raped in foster homes, kindness in the male form was enough. Money, riches, a house or at least a well-kept apartment, those were silly extras. She had just one thing on her list, kindness, and Frank was that in spades. He never failed in the big moments to see her, comfort her, and say the right words. He never made her feel doubt and most importantly, he never made her feel afraid. Until now. From behind Frank's back a knife appeared. It was not one they owned. It was, even in the dim light, foreign and sharp and cold.

"What the hell are you doing, Frank?"

His face had contorted into nothing but grotesque smile. He looked down a moment, took a deep breath, and then rushed her pregnant frame, her body crashing hard on the ragged bed, fresh blood on her lips and cheeks. He covered her mouth with quick force, tied her hands and legs with equal efficiency. Her struggles and muffled cries did not please him. He found this strange, he thought they would and he smoked a cigarette, trying to figure out his reaction. Then he picked up the knife he'd tossed on the floor as he rushed Elizabeth and put it in his back pocket. He stood over her. His green eyes were twinkly as ever and menaced by the smoke of a fresh cigarette. "Let me start with a great opening line: I am not Frank." He took a deep puff and then blew the smoke into her crying eyes. "Oh I look like him. And in a minute, I am gonna go nude and you're gonna see I *really* look like him." He bent down to her covered mouth and his alighted eyes froze hers. "*Exactly* like him. All over, baby...all over."

    She felt him undue the rope on her legs and then tie them apart. She tried to kick but he cut her legs so bad she acquiesced. He noted how calm he felt. This is all so unexpected, he thought. As he took off his pants, he said, "I first saw Frank at a coffee shop."

Maybe it was four months ago, maybe three, could have been six. Time had become diluted for him, folded into sleepless days and then without warning, dozy days. Whole weeks passing without peeling back the drapes, without doing a dish or eating anything that wasn't cold or delivered. Sometimes he felt like evil was falling from the sky onto him, just pressing him to the earth until it killed him or worse, buried him alive. He felt he had lived someone else's lifetime at the still young age of 35, if lifetimes were measured in psychological torment, doubt, erratic behavior and a fast realization that he was not only different but in fact, insane. His savings was running out. His unemployment had already run out. He wasn't easily amused like the rest of them. And the egotistical skyscrapers of the city disgusted him, lovers holding hands passing by banks which owned them disgusted him. Nothing was inviolate. He wanted to spit on God. Madness, he screamed. Sweet angry madness. The only honesty worth a party.

    Wouldn't it be nice to prove this meaninglessness true? If his emptiness had some kind of academic, quantifiable expression, he could go to hell in peace.

    "5 dollars even," said the checkout girl.

    He handed her a 10. "You know money is just a

theoretical absurd shackle," he said.

"5 dollars back," said the checkout girl.

———

He stopped listening to music, and that was what broke all feeling out of his heart. Music pushed so many other humane things through. Now that was gone, too, and his emptiness was highest at midnight when he craved fancy coffee and ironically, sleep. Coffee made the insomnia useful sometimes and there was a 24 hour joint that he could walk to. He took a shower, barely shaved, and then went out into the cool darkness. It should feel good to walk, he thought, but I feel nothing. A few couples passed by holding hands. It was as if they'd put a spotlight on him. Made him a freak. There's a transformation in me, he thought, and I don't understand....

And then he saw something that astounded him. That shook up every part of his soul. That would have disturbed anyone. His doppelganger turned into the light of the coffee shop, jamming to headphones and carrying a blue laptop bag. He wore a plain white t-shirt with black jeans and cheap black sneakers and even had the exact same badly shaved beard.

My god, he silently exclaimed, that's me! He's *me*.

Most human beings would have immediately sought out their doppelganger, just to get a closer look. To say simply, hello. But not him. His emptiness stopped him cold and sparked only an internal curiosity. He decided a tactical retreat was best for now, so he simply turned and went directly home, falling asleep as fast as the pills would let him. He wanted all the possibilities this afforded to rest, and when daylight woke him early, he had dreamed up a plan, and he headed out to drain his savings dangerously by buying some new, white trashy clothes, a blonde long-haired wig, a trucker cap that said Trucker Cap, and some black eyeliner. At the exact same time as last night, he took a shower, and then he put on his new disguise and left for the coffee shop. He tried to walk at the same pace he had the night before so things might repeat, and sure enough, into his vision his other appeared, blank stare ahead, headphones plugged in, blue laptop bag in tow. Exact same clothes as the night before.

This is going to be insane, he thought.

He felt a thrill standing behind his doppelganger, surreptitiously observing. He matched his headphones, but his didn't have any music playing. And his blonde wig, black eyeliner and ridiculous trucker cap made him look like, at best, a drug reject. The disguise was good because it was bad, and no one would want to look at him long enough to be looked back at. As he gazed at his other's shoes, he wondered if his mother was a bitch, too, or if he also had a terrible second grade romance, or if he slept with an ex best friend's sister as well. Imagination was fun again. Prurient with paranoia-soaked doom.

His other ordered a low-fat cappuccino and the barista said, "As usual, Frank."

Frank lifted his right earplug. "I am gonna change up one night."

"I will believe that when I make it," the barista said.

He is a boring chit-chatterer, he thought, and I hate those. But at least I got his name. And I know he sounds like me. Their voices were identical in every way.

Frank got his cappuccino and then camped at a table in the backroom, which had a few stray lonely people and stressed out college students, all staring at their phones and laptops. No one bothered to look around much. It was a *serious* late night crowd, beautifully self-absorbed. Frank sipped his coffee and then pulled out his laptop. I've got to get near him but not too near him, he thought. He had brought a book, **Melville: A Life Adrift**, and he instantly regretted it. No one reads anymore, at least on paper. I should have brought a computer. But he was an anachronism in life. His only computer was a home unit. He didn't even have a cell phone.

He stared at his book pretending to read, playing with the controllers on his CD Walkman once in a while so everyone would think he was jamming to tunes. He furtively tried to see what Frank was typing on his computer, but to no avail. He must be some kind of writer. He probably sucks, he thought. I suck. And then he got lucky. Frank's cell rang.

A picture of a beautiful, sad blonde appeared on the phone's screen. Frank took out his headphones and whispered, "Hey honey. Yeah, I know. But you know I can't sleep until I get this short story done. It's obsessing me...I love you. I promise not to be as late as last night. I promise...hey, now I feel challenged. You're getting pregnant sex when I get home, missy."

This is perfect for my imagination! he thought. His name is Frank, he's probably a fuck-up writer, and he's got a pregnant wife (or maybe he's trying to make her pregnant?) who is way too pretty for him. At this moment, all the darkness and evil he had felt crushing him began a march for truth at any cost. His heart overexerted with chaotic anticipation. Only one thought coalesced him: What does this mean *for me?*

2.

In the movies, he'd hire a private detective, or suddenly, ridiculously develop spy and burglary skills. But this was reality, and in reality he was a physically unexceptional and rapidly going bankrupt man. He wasn't suddenly going to be able to run across rooftops, or pick locks, or gain computer access to highly sensitive data. He was lucky that a lot of things were free on the Internet. And so he searched, and even paid for a transcript of all births from his hometown during his birth year. He had to make sure his mother hadn't lied to him. That he had been an only child, miserably fatherless and poor. He had to make sure this Frank was something more than an explainable, expendable twin. The investigation data which came back matched his own Internet searches: There had been no second, secret baby, no mysterious twin.

So now the search was about Frank's life, his zigs and zigs. But how was he going to get Frank's last name to make that happen? He ran around with complicated, silly plans to get this task done. Frank walked to the coffee shop, so no tag could be gotten, and given the nature of their impersonal city, Frank lived in a high rise, so no exact address could be easily obtained. All surveillance ideas seemed like fiction, like something out of a spy movie. And given the nature of his disguise, and the fact he was not trained for police/spy work of any kind, surveilling Frank beyond the coffee shop was just a bad idea. He'd inevitably screw up. Get detected. Spoil all of it. He had to find a better way.

Walking around the city, a better way walked past him. She had on a tight black mini-skirt and stained red top, and she reeked of everything cheap. "Hey brown sugar pie," he said. She turned. Her smile was as empty as her wallet. "I've got the easiest money you've ever made."

For a crack addict, Brandi was punctual.

I'm going broke faster than I can handle, he thought. He looked at his wallet. Soon it would be credit only, and he didn't have much of that in his life.

Brandi's slightly beat-up smile headed toward Frank. A practical joke on my twin, he had told her. That's the job. Get him to say his last name, because he hates it so. She told him the joke was lame, but it was his money, so.

He hoped Brandi wouldn't recognize him through his absurd coffee shop disguise as he watched it all go down.

"I know you, you're Frank Milton," Brandi said. "Yeah. You owe me money."

Frank nervously took off his headphones. "What?"

"You're Frank Milton," she said, uncomfortably louder.

"No I am not."

"Yeah you are. You still owe me 20 motherfucker."

The students and the sleepless souls and the barista were all starting to pay attention. Frank had sat in the main room tonight because of a crying baby dominating his usual backroom netherworld, and so this scene was full-on public with an audience.

Come on Brandi, he thought. Get this right. He'd given her a ripped 100 dollar bill and promised her the other half and a fresh one if she got his last name.

"I'm not Frank Milton."

"Show me your driver's license."

Frank looked around for help, caught the eyes of the barista, who handed over her latest creation while eying Brandi; she then made a beeline toward the situation. Her stocky hips wobbled together. Her newest tattoo was red and bright and fresh on her left arm. Her cheeks were chubby with sweat and her coffee scented hair was darkly stringy. "Hey you gotta go," she said.

"He owes me 20!" Brandi shouted. "Right Frank Milton?"

"I am not him!"

"I am getting the police lady if you don't go," the barista said.

"He's fuckin' Frank Milton and he owes me money," Brandi shouted at the barista.

"You gotta go!"

"I want to see his driver's license. Let him prove it bitch!"

Frank, exasperated, grabbed his wallet. He held it out to her and shouted, "Look! I am Frank Pagilton. See,

Frank *Pagilton."*

Brandi took a courtesy glance. Then she turned and walked out. Walked out with pride, he thought. For a cheap whore, she's sure got spirit.

———

He found Brandi twenty minutes later near the all-night newsstand. He had to do a real superman kind of change at a 24 hour donut shop before meeting her; the gym bag holding his disguise had seen better days, he noted. I should get a blue computer bag like him....

Brandi screwed up the name Frank gave her, but that didn't matter. She had been a good, dutiful whore, and that was something to be proud of, he told her. He gave her the money. And then he asked her to score him something important. "Meet me here tomorrow night. If you got it, I'll give you another hundred, my brown sugar plum."

Brandi looked at the money. "Hey Johnny bring that money baby. Bring it."

He smiled as he watched her go off into the night. I found the best 2 dollar whore alive, he thought.

Frank Pagilton, aged 35, currently unemployed, job history one of spotty inefficient management. Mother, Nancy Pagilton, nee Wiacek. Father listed as Brian Pagilton. Never lived at the same address with Nancy or Frank. Fatherless just like me, he thought. Frank married three years ago to Elizabeth Lee, aged 26 at the time. He likes'em younger. I wonder if he thinks they're weaker that way?

    Hasn't worked in a while, I guess he's following his dreams of writing and she's tolerating it. Elizabeth Lee's life, or what could be ascertained from his Internet prying, wasn't good. Broken girl from the start, wasn't she. I guess she settled for him, or he's a violent asshole and she needs violent assholes. Pretty, maybe pregnant, Elizabeth. As he sat in his cave, dark and underfed and virtually soundless, the echo of his echoless days made him feel tired and angry. He kept seeing Elizabeth's beauty. And he was sure Frank wasn't an asshole, and this gnawed at him. As he fell asleep, it occurred to him that, given this situation, an infinite number of scientific, even familial, possibilities, of actions and directions and meaningful exchanges, had been carved into something as simple as petty jealousy. But that is my mind, he thought. In it, wonder deteriorates into malicious focus.

Oh well. I wonder if Frank deteriorates, too. If I prick, does he bleed? Is my smile his collapse? I wonder about Elizabeth and what she means *to me*.

3.

Night one of his risky plan was a disaster. Frank didn't get up from his computer once. Night two, he got up twice to pee, but each time the table was blocked with pain in the ass patrons. Night three, night three he got lucky. The backroom was clear and Frank had to pee within minutes of sitting down. He glided by and dropped more than enough Rohypnol in Frank's tea.

    He sat and waited. It didn't take long. If the usual, physically oft-putting barista had been on duty, this would have been way riskier – if she had poked into the backroom and seen Frank, odds were she would have intervened and called Frank a cab or used his phone to find Elizabeth's number. But tonight, everything that could go right was going right. The new girl on duty was pretty and absent minded and had one of those sudden long and edgy lines all service businesses get from time to time. As Frank dazed, he pounced. Making out like he was his buddy, he put his computer away. "I told you not to drink," he said good-naturedly, and no one even noticed. Out the side door they went, right to his old Chevy. Frank went bye bye as he landed on the front seat.

He drove casually. He could get Frank into his apartment with little fuss. No one was up at this hour, and in his part of town, no one cared. He got him in, threw him on his bed, and then took his keys and wallet. He went to an all-night Superstore and got copies of all Frank's keys, and then had to put up with procrastinating students at the all-night copy shop. Then he headed home. He'd tied Frank up as a precaution, but he doubted he'd awaken for hours. And he was right.

Once home, he took a sip of water from the kitchen sink's tap, and then headed toward his bedroom. This would have all been better at a motel, but he was running out of credit and besides, motels have their own bad karma, right? Their own risks. Fuck it. What's done is done.

He undressed Frank. Everything about the process was slow, even erotic. He compared moles, wrinkles, scars. He ran his hands along Frank's skin. It was like he was discovering his self for the first time. And if anyone had been watching, they would have found it comical the way he dazed on Frank's penis. It was almost as if it were more important that their penises matched than their faces, their matching genitalia in both size and scope legitimized the phenomenon for him. It was official now that their cocks were a match! His mind felt on fire from observation. And as he took swabs from the inside of Frank's mouth, he did not wonder who Frank was. He wondered who he was. He felt a speeding realization that he'd always wondered this, that in the end, every failure was in response to this curiosity, to this unknowable idea. And now Frank was given to him as some kind of tool to explain or justify, a perfect copy to use as he saw fit: a control subject maybe, or maybe just a rehearsal stand-in, or maybe a slave sacrifice for a greater truth. Except Frank had a wife, didn't he? A pregnant, pretty wife. Frank was not alone. He gazed down at Frank's crotch and then his own. It took him awhile to figure out what he was feeling was just pure, unmitigated hatred, and nothing else.

―

It took two weeks for the test results to come back – he paid a helluva lot more than the regular price for such a quick turnaround. The letter informed him he had made a mistake. "Both DNA samples are identical," it said, "which means the samples given were accidentally from the same person. We cannot refund you for this error, but we are willing to offer you a discount on,"

He stopped reading. His ego and his imagination felt applause. I was right. I knew it! I think I see now I've always been right. This is all a grand process if you're right. A cold stage that's all mine. He sat down. I think I'll take up smoking, he thought. Maybe heroin next. Maybe crack. He laughed.

Time went by fast as his thoughts went by slowly. He didn't even realize he was walking now, out of his apartment, and it was 3 am. "I'm a powerful man," he said to the newsstand clerk as he handed him his cigarettes.

"5 bucks," the clerk said. He didn't stutter.

———

Frank's computer was password protected. He had to do a lot of research to find out how to bypass it, and in the process, he erased the drive. It was useless. I'll never get to read it, he thought. Never know if he was any good.

He wondered if Elizabeth and Frank were having fights. He was sure she wasn't happy finding out her loyal husband had been found passed out with an empty liquor bottle behind an unsavory bar. Computer and what little cash he had, stolen. He could imagine her yelling, imagine her pregnant nerves losing it on him, imagine Frank failing to back up his work and losing all his creativity.

    I should be the writer, he thought. I am making a true story anybody would kill for. It's a story of self-discovery and one of a kind genius. Of divine selection and truth. He lit a cigarette. Watch me now, baby, he laughed. Watch me now.

———

Rehearsal: Key works on building's front door, note the lobby cameras, note the camera in the elevator, note the camera in the hallway. Key turns lock in Frank's door. This is so fucking exciting. But don't go in. Just walk out the emergency exit. Heart is alive for good now.

On the night of the killing, he had to take a big chance: he had to bet on Frank not changing anything, on being his usual, cappuccino drinking, white t-shirt, black jeans, cheap black sneakers wearing self. Frank rarely changed his habits but still, things are only probable, not certain. He thought about how predictable he had been, how predictable his tastes and depressions and doubts and wardrobe had been until he saw Frank. Seeing myself released myself, he thought. I am my own surprise, I am my own satisfaction.

Frank left his building at the usual time, walking toward the coffee shop. The streetlights were semi-broken, but it appeared he had worn his usual late-night attire.

He waited 20 minutes and then casually unlocked the building's front door. He even stopped to check the mail, but then wondered if this had been a faux pas. Perhaps the cameras would see he had already checked the mail? Anyway, the damage was done. But what if the cameras aren't even working? What if they're broken or just for show?

Why hadn't I thought of that? Oh well, and out came a slim brunette in nurse's garb from the elevator. "Hey Frank, off again to write?"

"Yeah, just forgot some notes."

"Tell Lizzy I said hi. Good luck writing. You gotta let me read it."

"Will do," he said. When the elevator doors closed, he let out an inner fist pump. The camera couldn't see him joyful. But the camera could definitely see him.

———

"I guess you're wondering why," he said to Elizabeth as he put his pants back on. "A week ago I think I still couldn't...define why. There's no why on the surface. And I've never done anything remotely like it. Never even got a traffic ticket. But I suppose there's something in me that wants a completion of some sort. A proof of the limitation of my ability to care. I wanna know if I do this if it will mean more, and less, what I think it will. The word *why*, Elizabeth, is me, I guess."

Elizabeth was out of her body now. Her legs were lifeless, her eyes so terrified tears couldn't penetrate out anymore. The only things with life on her were her baby bump and heavy breathing, which seemed to be trying to force her to snap-in again, to fight, to live. He looked at her closely, at her rising breasts and round tummy. "If I felt joy at violating you, or in your suffering, then I'd know I was one person all my life. But I feel no joy. I feel nothing. I am just a certain person at this certain moment."

    He sat next to her on the bed. He held the knife. "I feel nothing. And now you will, too."

Frank had a recent history of blackouts. After all, he had been found drunk and completely in delirium behind a bar just 4 or 5 weeks ago. Moreover, the coffee shop alibi was nothing; it had no cameras in the backroom; he could have slipped out the side door, killed Elizabeth, slipped back in. What was clear was the camera in the hallway had him as the only person in and out of their 7th floor apartment. His DNA was all over Elizabeth and the immediate crime scene. And as he left, the elevator camera showed he had forgotten to clean all the blood off his neck. His white t-shirt was spotted with it. It was incontrovertible. Too easy. But too much to ignore.

    Frank Pagilton was guilty. The sentence was death by electric chair. Frank looked baffled on TV. He looked as if someone had stolen his being. He looked as if he believed in nothing except nothingness. He looked like his other.

4.

He made a list of all the humanity he felt in the aftermath. The crime was sensational and psychotic and got national attention. In fact, it got so much attention he had to escape to a new town with dyed hair and a well-groomed face. He hadn't thought about the press, and he was judgmental of the fact that he liked his bad deed being on television. I am a cheap popularity whore, he thought, and I like it. And this made him bitter.

    But for all the bitterness, he felt relief, too. He felt good even, so good, in fact, that it tormented him that he could tell no one. He took a measly job in a measly town and went back to the unexceptional life he had before Frank. He was always broke and always empty and very lonely. And the human condition presses for social contact, for release. For sharing its misery or just shouting its joy. It isn't enough to be right. You have to *tell* someone how right you are....

One day in the park, a homeless man of at least retirement age appeared in his line of vision. He took out a 20. Amazing, I am so poor yet even I had enough money to pull all this off. It's good to be in America, he thought, and he tore the 20 in front of the man. "Here's half. Sit down and listen to what I have to say, and you get the other half. I suspect you have nothing to lose but 5 minutes."

The homeless man took the torn bill. He sat down on the bench, his one bag crashing to the ground. It was full of cans and hell knows what else.

"Call me...call me *Frank*," he said. "Yeah. And I did something...well, I can't scientifically confirm that this was the only instance. I admit, I am romanticizing that this is the only instance. But we all romanticize and so my suspension of disbelief can be born here. Yes, be born!" He grinned. The homeless man made no expression. He held the broken 20 in a shaking right hand.

"I did something *perfect*. I mean, I did something so *perfect* it can't be improved upon. The perfect crime I made. The perfect murder. The kind Sherlock Holmes doesn't believe in. No one has ever done one any better. In all the history of man, mine was best – and it was easy. And doing something well, especially uniquely well, is a reward like no other. I destroyed myself in a perfect murder. And you know what: I also exonerated all my mediocrity, too. I exonerated all my mistakes, all my littleness in the universe."

He looked at the old homeless man. His blankness and his trembling had increased.

"Ask me," he ordered, "how I did all that?" The old man didn't utter a sound.

He shouted at him, "Ask me how damn it!" but the old man couldn't even manage a brief mumble, let alone a sentence. And then he just fled. Scared out of his mind by that maniac's green twinkled eyes.

"Disbelief is its own universe!" he shouted after the old man. He looked around. No one was near. Maybe I was jealous. Maybe I was insane. He looked around. Maybe that sky with the orange hue and sliver circles is beautiful. Maybe all that green and blue bouncing from that ocean in my dreams is timeless wonder. He looked around for faces, for sound, but there wasn't even an echo from the wind anymore. Call me *Frank*, he shouted to no one. Maybe her smile was too beautiful, maybe death doesn't collapse so nice. Maybe being right and insane are no different. And maybe, well, please for now on, someone, anyone, please call me Frank. Because

Frank was a good guy, right?

The Three Relationships of Eve

The lighting here was always bright in corners and then naughtily dark as the canvas spread out. A petite girl with dark hair and barely legal mouth stood against the jukebox, noticeably undressed and urgently fascinated at the choices – and then she turned and caught Jonah at the end of the bar. He had an endless cigarette going, a vague, smirking smile, and half a drink. His good looks were hard – exact without apology or room to add. And she loved his broad shoulders – she suddenly wondered if her climbing black skirt was going to be enough.

The bartender was cheerful, busty and usually interested in Jonah – either because he never tried to hit on her or because she was one of those that couldn't resist falling in love with bad decisions. In any event, she was the only female he exempted from advances and this annoyed her – Jonah enjoyed that part. But he left her alone mainly because he believed you never fuck the help at your main bar. No matter how great her tits were.

"She was a cat lover, this last chick," Jonah shouted; his eyes never matched his voice – they were incurably looking for more anywhere and everywhere. "She didn't want to leave me alone. And I found out she knows my boss! What are the odds I'd boink a cat loving sorority sister of *that* bitch?"

"So what did you do to get rid of this one," the busty bartender shouted back as she poured a pitcher.

Jonah lit up like a Christmas tree. "I took her out Friday night and ran over a cat." He laughed. His big sip was rewarding. "I said it was an accident, but said it like a dick, you know? And she couldn't get over that one. No way. Fucking brilliant, huh?"

Just now the young girl near the jukebox pulled her black skirt up a notch and Jonah saw her smiling. He smiled back and her top seemed to get a little tighter. She hadn't said a word to him yet but oh that smile of his was handsome and life felt turned on and great. And it would turn out that she loved cats, too, and this made Jonah grin a lot. It's gonna be another good one, he thought.

―――

It was Friday and Paul took Eve to Rose's Rocker, a chic, overpriced nightspot which trailed along the Fort Lauderdale evening strip without a thought in its head. It featured a trippy water bar, slutty yet classy waitresses, and lots of space covered in loudness and smoke.

Eve actually disliked this bar, so it was sad Paul chose it to impress her. She hadn't moved to Florida last year looking for trendy places like this. She had just wanted a sunny change. But hell, she did appreciate that he would spend his average salary on overpriced places to please her. Not to impress, mind you – to *please.*

Paul watched Eve slowly leave their table now, admiring her curves as they busted tight into her jeans while her red hair curled downward, her breasts large yet strapped down well, barely bouncing as she walked the long hallway to the ladies' room. Eve had a centerfold's body – the kind of body that was primal and life giving, and Paul adored every part of it, especially her curly, passionate red hair – she was a southern girl with southern hips, southern wild hair, and white skin so untouched she looked ten years' younger than 36 – young beyond her years was how she described herself – and she appeared conspiratorially girlish when she smiled, which Eve did a lot because smiles, she believed, promoted strength.

But she didn't smile now as she walked down the long hallway to the ladies' room – she hated long hallways, especially this one with all its noise and crowded bodies. And thinking about sitting with Paul as he alternated between annoyed and curious put a tense imbalance over her nerves.

Eve suddenly felt sick and guilty and angry and the goddamn lights got dimmer with each step, and a sharp sliding pain started running up her side – God I feel so sick, she thought, and she held her hand over her mouth, fighting the urge and trying desperately to reach the bathroom door – instead she ran right into it and collapsed on the neon studded carpet. Other girls coming and going saw it all and laughed. A few asked if she was OK. Eve shook her lovely red hair No to all their noise and tried to shut out the awful music as she slunked down into the ground, her small hands made into fists, her eyes trying to blur out the whole spectacle so she wouldn't feel so dizzy.

Paul found her a full hour later, sitting there in the blur. He had been shocked when he boozily realized she'd been gone this long. Truthfully, he'd enjoyed the pressure drop of her absence.

Eve didn't look up. "I was just relaxing," she said – and instantly thought: Why did I say *relaxing*?

"What the hell are you talking about? Didn't you think I was worried?" Paul shouted. Her lie was troubling but what really shook him was his lie – he hadn't been worried at all.

———

Paul drove only American cars and Eve mentioned this in bed from time to time – and it irked him. Was it a shot? And why mention it *in bed?*

Hell what did she *want* anyway? A man with German cars? Japanese cars? Fast rich cars, probably. He tried to be a good guy to Eve, agreeing with her all the time as they lay in bed that she was strong, that she was special, that she had overcome the abuse, the distrust. The poor-choosing doubt. But when they made love, sometimes he felt she was absent – caught up in violence and memory – and somehow resenting *him* for it. Lately, he wondered if he said the right, kind things about her awful past out of love, or just passive-aggressive resentment.

Maybe I say them out of doubt, he thought. Nervousness at her doubt – at her moments of picking a withdrawal to prove she could withdraw. In the big moments, he felt she chose selfishly and poorly, but hell, it wasn't her fault. Because after what had been done to her so many times, it could never be her fault, but still....

And Paul told everyone that gave him that doubtful look that none of it was her fault – the way she is, he'd say – how could anyone recover from so many violations as a child? But still....

That's the big problem, he thought, I just have too much to say after I know it's not her fault, and he looked at Eve as they passed by restaurants and asked her blankly if she wanted to eat something; he looked at her as they passed by churches and hospitals – he wanted to ask if he should stop at any of these – maybe one of them could help.

Eve didn't look at Paul much anymore when they rode together, but she did care for him. He had humor and easy charms and she'd felt safe when she first met him. Her life brightened and their intimate moments were full of wisdom for a while and she wrote a paper for her counseling masters about the positives of women embracing safety as a sexual feature in men. Not rescue, mind you, not protection – safety. Safety was a giving thing, not an act of self-importance. Paul had been a giving thing. At first, anyway.

But then nausea set in – just exploded from nowhere like bad weather can, and sex with Paul became dirty, or wrong, or just impossible for a time, and when she and Paul's relationship inevitably started to break apart, Eve went to one counseling session with him. Just one. Paul wondered how a counseling major could give up after only one session.

But he marched on anyway. For months. And now she'd collapsed in a bar. She had looked so calm when he found her lying on that trendy carpet. He drove a little faster, thinking about *the just one counseling session* and about how calm she looked – and Eve stared at the street signs and brake lights...Paul's sweet – *mostly anyway*, she thought – but he doesn't make a lot of money – not that that should matter...but it does matter – but it isn't the money that matters...it's...it's his lack of ambition. That's the *thing*!

Yes, she decided, it's the ambition-lessness of him that bothered her. It was the way he sold himself short all the time – because wasn't that selling her short, too? She needed something from her man and ambition was behind that something – hell, it had to be. It might be my strength, she thought, to accept that money is an issue for the right reasons – it's OK for a strong woman to admit this.

Paul pulled into Eve's driveway. She got out first and, seeing her sad, blank stare in the moonlight made him feel sad for her, so he hugged her. But Eve wasn't sad – she just wasn't there and the hug felt like a violation – it felt *unsafe* and alone. "I don't want to talk about it," she said, her Georgia accent cruelest on the word *don't*.

"I know it's been hard, you know," Paul said in her bedroom, "what you went through. But I am not your stepfather, Eve. Even if we have the same goddamn name. You look at me lately like...like you're trying to find him or something else. I don't know what you want and fuck – this isn't my fault, either, you know."

Eve sat at the end of her bed, undressing without looking his way. She took off her large bra and still didn't look his way. She wants me to hug her, Paul thought, but distrusts the hug. Fucked, isn't it....

Eventually, Eve tried to enjoy her cats and called out love and kisses to the three of them. Her cats made her feel safe. Even when she was a child and nothing had helped, they always helped. She pulled on a pajama top and then climbed into bed.

Paul took off his pants and shirt and joined her. They stared at the dark for a while and Eve petted her cats and then she talked about how she hated that long hallway at the bar so much – and it must have been a bad liquor mix that made her sick. That makes sense, doesn't it?

Paul agreed with her until she fell asleep.

James worked in finance. He did well, too. And he hugged Eve now as she curled up next to him, wine and cats in tow. "His name was Paul," she said. "I remember that long awful hallway in his house – he inherited that house and let it go to hell. It was always filthy. We tried and tried but we could never get it clean. My mother hated that house." She took some sips of wine. Her voice became disturbingly monotone. "I guess it wasn't that long of a hallway to my bedroom, but I remember it as being very long. It was like it stretched out for miles and it pushed him away and pushed me back. At first, it made me feel safe from him. He was everywhere and it made him farther away in my mind, you know? I was coping. But after a while I could hear him walking and it made his footsteps take forever, so I started to hate that hallway with everything else in that house."

Eve sipped her wine and then moved her head tight against James' chest. She started to tell him more, but he stopped her out of kindness – he didn't need the brutal details and this touched her. She almost told him there had been other rapes besides her stepfather. She almost told him she loved him. But he hadn't said that yet, so....

It's on him to say it, she thought. That's the way it's supposed to be between men and women and she held him tighter, almost like she was trying to squeeze it out of him, and James finally had to slip away because she was hurting his car-accident damaged back. But he felt guilty about stopping her, so he got a fresh glass of wine and whispered gushy sweet things to her, and soon she was holding him tight as hell again – she didn't seem to notice his winces. I guess she needs it, he thought. He took some pain pills and then whispered he loved her.

"I love you, too," she whispered back. "If I had met you in my 20's, I would have gone to college sooner."

They had sex all night, and the pain pills mostly worked.

When Paul got downsized, Eve made him a special dinner and bought him his favorite beer. But by the third week of unemployment he was depressed as hell, and Eve was, well – *outwardly kind*. She had sex with him and made him big meals. She told him it would work out. But when he asked her to take a trip so he could get away from his saddening life for a few days, she told him she couldn't. Now it was true that she had vacation time to use, and she was between semesters at graduate school and she saw that he needed to go someplace – *any place* – because he was dying inside. But something inside her just said No. "I need my vacation time to go see my mother at Christmas," she told Paul. And this was true. Her mother was important – even with all the bad memories she let happen. And Paul should understand that she wanted to help him but she had responsibilities and family was important and....

There were a lot of ands, but Paul didn't hear them. He just nodded. Eve was being oh-so-reasonable as she drifted away. And casual. And later, she causally whispered I love you to Paul – and it was at that moment he knew it was just about over.

In a month, Eve watched passively as Paul got really drunk...and then there was a fight...and then she claimed the next day that the fight had showed he was some *thing* she couldn't let in her life again.

Hell, truthfully – Paul couldn't remember the fight. He remembered being sad and then angry that she wouldn't take a trip with him – sad and angry with her in general and maybe the fight got worse than he believed, but he never got violent. He was sure of that. He wasn't a violent person, but the next day she looked at him as if he'd hit her, or worse. Before he could even buy makeup flowers, her cell phone number was changed. Her locks were changed. She was never going anywhere with him again. She fixed in her mind what he looked like drunk and angry...that's what this was about now, she proclaimed. Not his unemployment or lack of ambition...not his fated empty wallet. No, it was just the way he looked that night and she had to make sure that look *never* touched her again.

Eve cried the first day of the breakup. But not after that. A few months later, she found a new job in Virginia and everything about the move felt like strength, felt like triumph – felt like *victory*. And not one friend of hers bothered to ask her victory from *what*?

Jonah wore all black tonight and enjoyed, more than usual, looking at the busty bartender. But as usual, he did not hit on her. And the crowd was jumpier than normal for a Thursday night. Too much jukebox and fallen heroes in the air, but hell, a good looking girl sat next to him and took the unusual ice breaker of buying him a drink. He looked down her tits and smiles and felt that delicious cruel fire to take all of her forever.

They'd end up dating for at least two months, he thought, because she was hot enough to last that long. Such nice tits. Natural, too – just like her smile! And when it came time to get rid of her, he invented a "genius plan": he passive-aggressively played off her fears of disappointing him, as well as her fear of ending up a husbandless-woman like her mother, and then mixed both of these with her youthful sincerity toward Catholicism – the first two helped him get out of her goddamn pregnancy. Fucking vodka had told him to go bareback! And when she got the abortion, mostly for him – well, the Catholic part helped him destroy her: Jonah told her she'd misunderstood him. How could she not have *understood*? He'd wanted the baby! *Their* baby!

"Murderer! You murdered our child you bitch!" he screamed.

That night Jonah shouted to the busty bartender, "Best one yet."

It took a few months to feel fully moved into Virginia, but by the start of her third month Eve was ready to meet James – and his luxury became a wonderful part of her new life. She was now a Virginia woman through and through in her mind and James was a successful man – he didn't get downsized – he bet on whether others would. And he was good looking, too, if a little pudgy, but that was OK and he liked to smile a lot and Eve took on her new counseling job with the heart of a woman celebrating.

Lying in James' upscale condo, watching him sleep, she couldn't think of any reason not to marry him. He was kind, he was confidant, he had a great job, and as she snuggled closer to him, he sure felt safe.

Safer, anyway.

In foxholes, people show their true colors. And relationships are foxholes.

–That's what Eve's ex-Marine stepfather used to tell her the morning after a fight with her mother. He also said her mother was a coward. But usually, the bastard didn't say much to her. He had control without words and he knew it and he enjoyed her knowing it. He also enjoyed killing her with smiles. In one of her college papers, she described him as fire that constantly burned her past.

The professor liked that a lot.

Eve didn't want to believe that getting married was a foxhole – a constant test of one's character. In truth, she didn't want to think about it. But all she did was think about it because she was closer to 40 now than 30 and James loved her, even though the fact she hadn't been married before and was distant on children made him uneasy. He had been married once. Had a kid – a daughter named Lisa. And he was raised by good Protestants who believed that a woman that hadn't gotten married by her mid 30's and didn't have children on her radar was somehow incurably off. But Eve looked 28 to him and she was kind and beautiful, so he took those to heart, rather than the superficial judgments of his family and peers. And this worked well enough until the *little things* started – stuff Eve just whiffed on like his work engagements, which she either ignored or attended with mediocre awareness. And there were Christmas gifts ill thought about – and *too much* enthusiasm when he was paying for nice things – which of course was *always*. But then, then came Lisa's recital.

It was no big deal – just a junior high music thing. But to James, these things should be treated like a big deal, so he decided to throw a family party afterward, a big affair with all the in town relatives – he even would invite his ex-wife's new boyfriend. He assumed Eve would help him out with all the planning madness.

"I've got class," she said. "It's important for my doctorate study I started. You know that." She stood motionless, looking as if *he'd* hurt her somehow.

James rubbed his beard and stared ahead. This sort of answer had been creeping in a lot lately. "It's just one night."

Silence.

"I'll make some pies," she said, "chocolate is Lisa's favorite."

She bit her lip slightly. "But I can't make it that night. Maybe the last half of the party and...."

James looked around Eve's apartment, which was always being cleaned but was never clean. Furniture was always in the process of being moved around. It was always being something, he thought, it really wasn't. And it smelled of cats and too much dust. "You don't have to come if you need to study," he said evenly.

Eve barely looked at him. "I'll drop off the pies the night before, Ok?"

James didn't answer. He studied her for a moment as their relationship free-falled in his mind – memories crashed and cracked and then somehow snapped back together in the end, forming the first drips of clarity for him. And suddenly his chest felt pushed in and his stomach felt like someone had taken a corkscrew to it. Eve was now one of those things he knew without fully accepting yet, and the inevitable blows of that were starting their assault.

He answered, "Ok," and for the rest of the night, James tried to keep all his answers to her that short. He mostly succeeded. And Eve resented him for this, but she didn't say so. And he noticed that. He was noticing everything, and he turned to one side to watch her sleep as he thought about things, but her gentle breathing and the way she girlishly curled up as her dreams rolled on by gave him no comfort as the hours passed, and when he saw the sun bleeding through the curtains, he realized how tired he was going to be.

So over the next few weeks, James started to eat a lot more than he should, and it usually made him sick. He started falling asleep with whiskey on his breath and waking up just three hours later for work. And he worked later and later.

In relationships, James was a slow-thinking and slow-judging man – especially this time because he felt real sorrow about Eve's past. But after over a month of this hell he showed up at Eve's place. "I've got to end this," he said. Every piece of him lacked sleep. His skin was dry and rough. His eyes were steady, though – he was the type of man who didn't look away when giving bad news.

Earlier in the day he had returned the engagement ring he'd almost given her. Handing it back to the merchant made him feel sicker – but once James was in gear, he was all business. And he didn't waste time telling Eve why it was over. "I don't know who you are, I really don't – thought I did but.... I do think you're a marriage counselor who's never been married. Who has no children, who –"

Eve screamed. She was in tears. Why the hell was he saying these things? James had always been so kind – so *accommodating*. Such an understanding gentleman. Selfless – as much as anybody could be, anyway. So she just never imagined he had such self-protective, sharp cuts in him.

But James felt he had no choice. Because he had realized that he was never going to be enough. Thinking about the night he first told her he loved her, he said cryptically, "There are not enough pain pills, Eve."

James immediately tried to say something better than that, but realized quickly there wasn't anything better to say, so he sighed and bowed his head; he'd hated saying this painful stuff to her, but it had to be done. He wished he could say something nice – something profound that makes everything OK – like they do in the movies. But the dirty fact was *he* needed to get this out now, *he* needed to tell her the unvarnished truth before the relationship wrecked him completely; his best hopes had simply run out of time.

"I think you use, Eve," he whispered. "The truth is I think

you're a user. I just can't blame you for it."

Those words took the last of the relationship out of James, and he suddenly felt tired as he stared at Eve's damp, Irish green eyes. Truthfully, he felt more sadness for her than love and probably always had. And even though their relationship was over, he still wanted to save her – or at least be something positive for her. He wanted to reach over and touch the tears away from her pale, smooth cheeks. But a hug and a kiss and eternal forgiveness, for all the kindness and romance they'd bring, couldn't change her, would never change her – and he'd just end up unappreciated and less in the end if he stuck around. I really gotta get out of here now, he thought – and the front door opened, "Goodbye Eve," – and then it closed.

James never came back for any of the clothes or jewelry he left behind. Eve eventually realized that he could afford to lose them.

Eve cried a lot over James. And then came gusty Chicago. It seemed like the perfect change, but it turned out making friends there was hard. And she was never one to mind winter, but she hated Chicago's brand of it – it was violent and just took the fight out of people. This was a cold, cold place, and she couldn't connect with anyone. She mostly stayed at home, sipping wine and spacing out – sorta slunked away like she was nothing to be seen – similar to her mini-breakdown in the bar that night. Winter here was definitely a mistake.

But the summer got better – she made a few friends. And she started stealing time at her apartment building's pool. She especially loved night swims – midnight dalliances when she was the only one alive and she dove into moonlight splashes now like a happy, simple high school girl. Her hippy body fit snugly in her green one piece as she swam off thoughts and uneasiness. And it was soft when she floated and stared up at the stars – what were left of them, anyway, in the big city sky. Eve had always loved astronomy – the romantic physics of it. It was the only science that offered more wonder than facts. Two teenagers who'd snuck out to be cool stopped near her, cursing and trying too hard. Eve gave them an adult stare and they moved on.

    Alone again, she resumed floating under the few stars left, and sometimes her head fell beneath the water and a few waves lightly passed over her eyes...when she rose above them, she thought of Paul and their final fight...she'd given him the booze and then brought up how unhappy she was that he wasn't trying more...trying more for *what* he wondered because she never answered a job or money or...she fell underneath the water again and then rose up with thoughts of James. She still missed James. He was such a successful, caring man – but he wanted her to match his idea of things too much – and his daughter's recital was a manipulative test, she was sure. And James didn't understand what her No really meant – in a healthy relationship, to say No to something in particular is to say Yes to the relationship as a whole, and if he couldn't see that – what could she have done? He'd be just a taker if he couldn't see that – and he'd called *her* a taker! She was a woman recovered from takers! Takers would never understand a positive No and she swam some more and floated around to the ends of the pool, staring at the wandering clouds and the imprecise moon before finally going inside. She was worn out and just wanted some sleep.

    But she couldn't sleep. Between half dreaming and half insomnia, deeper thoughts and fears were always around, playing devil's advocate, casting doubt on her testimony – she was 39 and trying to fall asleep in the smallest, least-furnished apartment she'd lived in since her mid-20's, and life was being pushy tonight and selling the classic question: Is this just true or is it *the truth*? Am I right about them or wrong about me? And it was always so close, the ingrained terror – she always lived under the threat of being small, scared, dominated and hearing footsteps down a long hallway. It never got so far away that she couldn't just have it invade, make her cry or make her determined not to cry – which might be worse, she thought. She wished she could fall asleep as easily as she could remember the bad things – she pulled one of her cats closer and eventually she had all three purring and seeking attention and this was good enough to fall asleep to tonight. But it couldn't work forever. And sleepless nights make you do things. They just make you do so many goddamn things....

———

"Paul was his name," Eve said to the stranger next to her. "He was a monster."

Eve pressed the stranger's arm for a moment and then took a big sip. This bar was new to her and pleasantly dark tonight and the music, although too loud, was at least disco-fun and this man, he seemed to embrace something and that made him interesting. He felt a little dangerous, too – but maybe she was in the mood for dangerous. Sometimes you just needed to do something – *anything*, you know?

"There's so much you never know, you know?" Eve said, her tiny lips painted bright red tonight. Her smiles had a little protest to them. "My other Paul was nice enough – like I told you, but I just couldn't.... Why'd he have to lose his job or get drunk that night? Why was his name *Paul*?"

"My name's not Paul," the stranger said.

Eve stared ahead. The people behind her started to rock her senses a bit, but then their drunk noise left and the song playing became softer. "I used to bartend. But I'm a professional woman now." She laughed at this for a second but then shifted coolly to, "I'm a strong woman and I got over James' indifference. He was an unfair person, I think. In the end, he didn't understand that I couldn't say *Yes* to whatever he needed whenever he needed it. He didn't understand and...."

Time was now blending into the music and the booze, and Eve talked herself into shouting for another drink. "I guess it's not about the past, it's about how you *reframe* the past." She swayed to the happy music. "You just have to be careful and keep looking at the same time." She swayed some more. "I don't even know what I am trying to say, but you understand, right?"

Eve drank most of two more drinks and chatted into her stranger's encouraging silence, finally deciding that her instincts were fine, that in the end this was all just a process and yeah, she missed James, just like she missed Paul sometimes, but you move on and she was strong – she'd gotten over her past before and relationships were not foxholes. They didn't exist to push people into true colors; they existed to help people into better colors. And it was a good thing that James was gone, she decided – he was too much of a taker and better to find that out sooner rather than later. And it was great – just amazingly, incredibly great that this was all gonna be new now. She looked at the stranger's eyes and he was hard and masculine, confident – I think I feel safe with this guy, she thought, and he sure does *listen...*she was determined to trust her instincts. A strong woman trusts her judgment. That's what they try to take away first, you know.

I have to trust myself again, she thought, as she clasped her hands together. And this guy's got great broad shoulders and he bought me the sweetest drink here...and the lights over the jukebox, well even they were winking now. Everything was suddenly breathing again and Eve threw a smile the stranger's way and said, "Here's a tidbit about me: I have three cats that I love."

"My name is Jonah," the stranger said, and he thought: This is gonna be fun.

Cruel and unjust in the afternoon

It was noon and she bored him. It was time for this to not end well.

Chris could feel the disdain notching up now and it made him think about the irony of his home; he lived in one of those modern houses where every wall was made of glass. His mother used to tell him people in glass houses shouldn't throw stones. But that's all he ever did to human beings – especially women – one judgement after another, highlighting the faults and pushing out the pain, as if he wasn't also affected by the same sickness. But Chris would admit that not only was he just as ill – he was the worst person he knew. Nevertheless, she bored him now and not even the way she wore her red bikini tight and nice all the way down could change that.

"You're not very bright," he said, and for the first time in an hour, she stirred from her lazy haze on the couch. It was an expensive black-leather couch; everything in this house was expensive, in the impersonal way that inherited money creates – a lot of taste, but none of it Chris'. If you asked Chris, he'd tell you he didn't have any taste. Or feeling. And he stared for a moment through the surrounding glass – life was hot smoke out there to him, with a beach on fire and an ocean more cruel and beautiful than usual boiling over.

"You are pretty but not very bright and so, this cannot continue. Frankly Tina, you bore me. And I am sure I bore you. But my money does not. Money cures boredom, but not forever. And a particular beauty is only so enticing until you have tasted it. And since I have, well, tasted you...our time is over now." Chris knew the proper tone he used was worse than if he just talked like a regular person. It made his words seem clinical as opposed to personal – diagnosis, not opinion. Why do I do this? he thought. Why don't I just say, Hey baby, it's me, not you? She's crying and throwing things and I just sit here...because I don't care.

Chris looked at his watch. "I have to go now. I have to be at the university in an hour." He stood and smiled and this made Tina cry and rage even more, but the smile wasn't aimed at her. It was at the waiting group of college professors who were all excited to hear him read some of his verse. Chris was a poet. And if you asked him how that happened, he'd tell you this: Human beings must be very stupid.

****

Stephanie was the one in the crowd of folding chairs Chris noticed. There was a softness to her that he found irresistible. And she had the kind of wry smile that made her more beautiful when she showed it. She tied her long blonde hair professionally in back, but a few strands still playfully fell over her grey business jacket. And that jacket was a lie because she had an elegance that cried out for gowns and twirls on dance floors surrounded by champagne. And her eyes, brown and alert, were the type of eyes that tell you right away the IQ of a person – and there was no doubt hers was high. There were so many pretty girls in the world, but so few that were quick, and fewer still that had a mysterious quality around their smiles, and puzzles of thoughts in their eyes. Chris had two types: Beautiful and dumb, beautiful and smart. But there was one more he ran into once in a while: Beautiful, smart and unknowable – and it was that last that wrote the poems in his head. And he hurt them the most. But they were the best fuel and all Chris could notice in this room was Stephanie – an hour ago he'd broken a girl's heart, but he didn't even know her name now. He didn't know Stephanie's name yet, but he hungered to know her. Who are you, you pretty blonde thing? he wondered. I *need* to know – even though I will fail....

"Thank you all for coming," Chris said and looked down at page 24 of his book, *Sociopaths buy better flowers.* He put his stylish specs on, but took them right off. He made his eyes seem as if they were looking at a blur, but all they saw was Stephanie. He said:

> She walks by me and around me
> Wasteful daughter from a broken home
> So blonde and soft but not free
> She gives away too much
> and is always owned
>
> She walks by me again and around me
> Her skin faultless and her figure young
> She is beautiful and a lady

> Unknowable enough for a ballad
> and a country song
>
> Suddenly she stops and I think she sees
> That I want to save her so...
> Corny moons and morning daisies
> I'd give
> but I have no soul
>
> And now she starts again to walk by
> but this time I pull her near –
> As I look into those dark brown eyes
> I see only myself
> and that's what she should fear

When Stephanie was the one who raised her hand to ask what verse this was from, Chris smiled and thought, The gods I don't believe in must be with me today. He looked at Stephanie now with an intensity that was creepy but also, alluring, because it showed such interest. "It's something I just started to work on," he said.

After the reading was done, he cornered Stephanie near the bad coffee. In fifteen minutes, Chris had a first date. He went home and wrote a title for a poem: *It's time for it to happen all over again.* And then he got very drunk, very fast.

****

Chris was surprised when Stephanie agreed to go on an overnight cruise with him after just three dates. Separate cabins, of course. For whatever reason, Stephanie had decided that things with Chris should be taken "slow" – and that should have triggered the boredom clause of the relationship, but it actually made him feel relieved. It was 8pm now and the deck was mostly clear of people and Stephanie was dressed in an elegant purple dinner gown – the kind of ornery, classy clothing he'd imagined on her when he first saw her sitting in that academic kill-room. They were about to have a stylish and expensive late supper. But now they were leaning over the rail, looking at the fast moving dark ocean.

"I'm just making my dimes to spend my pennies/grooving like a skinny snake on a summer cruise/enjoying the little fish-ies."

"What the hell was *that*?" she asked.

"I made it up as a kid. My family dragged me on cruises a lot."

"It sounds like you didn't like cruises very much."

"I hated them."

"Then why did you invite me on one?"

Chris stared into the ocean so intensely now Stephanie wondered whether he had forgotten all about her – he seemed powerless against some disturbing personal revelation happening in real time in his head.

Why the fuck did I invite her *here*? Chris thought. He invited her for Thai food on their first date even though he hated it. He picked out a movie for their second date, even though it didn't appeal to him. On their third date, he invited her over to his place for dinner and that had ended in a good solid kiss and nothing more. He had made sure – at least his subconscious had, that both of them remained sober. He actually gave her soda without even asking. And now he was on a cruise ship full of childhood trauma.

"We should go eat," he said. And he made terrific conversation through dinner. He even took her out on the dance floor and found a verve and sweet-release he had never known before in his steps –

the circling lights seemed to just jump on the disco beats' shoulders and clap – and Stephanie was all smiles as they sweated and grooved. And then they drank some more whiskey and that made them sweat and groove some more. But not once while he did all this did he stop thinking: What the fuck am I doing *here*?

Later that night, lying in a lonely bed, Chris thought about how on their movie date, they'd run into one of Stephanie's exes. He had a man bun and his date was almost as tattooed as him. The awkward conversation that ensued didn't interest Chris at all – but the change in Stephanie's eyes did. They almost squinted. And Chris was sure that she was doing her best in her heart to feel bad about this guy. To *feel* anything. He was sure Man Buns didn't mean a goddamn thing – but she wanted him to, because for her it was better to feel something false than nothing.

I wish I had that kind of hope in my heart, he thought. It must be something to be that human.

****

The date tonight started with another movie neither wanted to see and then stopped at a karaoke bar. Stephanie loved to watch the embarrassed expressionism such a place thrived on and Chris didn't mind watching bad singers attempt *Total Eclipse of the Heart*. A good amount of booze helped things seem fun, and the loudness precluded conversation – and that's probably why Stephanie suggested they stop here. The relationship had hit that point where Stephanie had to decide if sex was going to happen or not. Over the past few weeks Chris had been mostly fun – full of humor but also, insight. She marveled at the way he seemed to instinctively know things about her. In fact, she'd normally have jumped into bed with a man who seemed so in sync with her – but there was something cold about Chris when he did this. He didn't seem empathetic. He made her feel like she was sitting on a metal examination table. It was interesting being a patient since he gave answers – but she wanted to be a girlfriend. And so she thought now: Where do I take this?

Chris intensely watched the crowd, and this allowed Stephanie a moment to examine him. He seemed always to understand something from a situation – a vulnerability, a truth, that others missed. It was easy to sit here and pretend to have a good time and not notice all the pedestrian, social fear on display. But he seemed to notice all of it for what it was and yet, it didn't seem to affect him. Stephanie wondered if *she* affected him.

Who the hell is he? she wondered. Chris' insights and candor made him seem close and yet, she didn't really have any idea if he was close. Stephanie felt like a cop and Chris was the perp: She was looking for clues, but more importantly, lies. There was a loud voice shouting to get away – but if Chris was an accident waiting to happen, she couldn't look away. There was something very familiar about him and then suddenly, he wasn't like any man she'd allowed herself to date. Why was it all so fucking confusing? Wasn't it supposed to be fun!

The bad singing fought against the encouraging yells now. It was loud and silly here and Stephanie wondered: Should I sleep with him tonight? Or should I just leave this safely in the friend-zone? And which guy would I be sleeping with – the familiar one, or the alien?

"What song are you going to sing?" Chris asked.

"I don't sing."

"Come on! Just one."

Stephanie shook her head.

"Well what would you sing?"

Stephanie was shocked her answer was so automatic. "You're always a woman to me."

Chris smiled and then turned his eyes toward the microphone stand, imagining Stephanie singing that Billy Joel song. Would she sing it hoping he felt those lyrics about her? Or would she twist it into a first-person narrative – singing it like a broken down protest – *I should always be a woman to you!*

Funny thing was, Stephanie was thinking the same thing. And maybe this unity of thought clinched it, because when their eyes met now her hand reached over his and all that bad noise faded away.

"The sooner you pay for these drinks the better," Stephanie said.

Chris often leaned toward rough and quick when it came to sex, but making love to Stephanie was a surprisingly slow experience; he found himself closing his eyes as he guided his hands along her warm skin. He undressed her with care and it surprised him how often he stopped his sexual hunger just so he could kiss her.

The moonlight bounced all through his house now as they rested tightly against one another on his couch. Things had started here, moved to the bedroom, and somehow returned to where it began. The unfinished wine glasses that had been a pretense to passion were still on the coffee table.

"My dad did business with yours," Chris said. "When he was alive, that is. Now, he probably just does business with Satan. I'm sure they get along."

Stephanie breathed slowly against his chest. "Your dad was a prick, too?"

"I guess they all are. That's why we're fucked up. At least, that's a pretty lie, isn't it?"

She laughed. "I hate knowing I am all daddy issues."

"So outside of dating trust fund poets, you like those greasy hipster idiots to date?"

She laughed. "Yes."

Chris looked into her eyes. "So you...Miss Elegance herself, educated professor of literature. Lover of Shakespeare – dates those idiots?"

Stephanie laughed again.

"Well at least they aren't Daddy, are they?" Chris said. "Name three things you admire/want in a man."

The first two didn't even register for Chris because the last one was so intriguing. *Ambition*. He sat up, charged with curiosity.

"Ambition. You say you want a man with ambition and yet, you date Man Buns who buys an overpriced computer – and talks about shit over it while drinking overpriced coffee – while he gets a 100,000 college degree in liberal studies that will pay him enough to consider being a waiter."

"And what's your point?"

"You're afraid to be known, girlfriend."

"Why?"

"Because these relationships will always fail your admire-test. You know they're doomed. That's why you take them in and bathe them."

"So who do you usually date?"

This question intrigued Chris, because she hadn't asked very much about him in the three weeks they'd been dating. She had enormous curiosity, but it was turned inward at this point in her life, and so she was content to hear his observations – observations he thought were obvious, but she seemed to like them – so he kept them up.

Chris got up and sat on the post-modern, thin – what he called "bullshit art-chair" that faced the couch. "I think I usually date you. When I am not dating you, anyway."

"I don't get it."

"Well, sometimes I date the commercial and sometimes I date the program. The last girl was the commercial. You're the program."

"I feel so *honored*," Stephanie said.

"I didn't mean it to piss you off. I just mean that…I am thinking about patterns lately. You know, people following little scripts, etc. And we're all fucked and I wonder how you get out of them. Is it hard work, self-analysis, personal inventory. Deep thought. Self-empathy. Or is that all bullshit and the only way anyone gets any hope is by getting a lucky, random disruption?"

"Explain."

"No." Chris got up and looked at the dark beach through the surrounding glass. "I like the ocean," he said. "Because it can be beautiful while still being cruel. Afternoon is usually when I am at my cruelest, for whatever reason."

"Chris, I don't know what you're talking about."

"I went to a psychiatrist Stephanie. Last year. Went to several, actually. I don't feel anything and I know what that diagnosis is but what I really wanted to know is if there was hope. Funny huh? I mean, I despise people all day long for their pathetic little sad worlds and here I am – paying a shit ton of money so someone with a college degree can tell me I'm going to be ok. Sad isn't it?"

"You think you're a bad person?"

"You think you're a bad person, don't you?"

"Yes."

"Narcissistic?"

"Yes."

"And yet, I bet – I just *bet* you think you're the best friend anyone could have."

Stephanie's eyes closed in thought, and her stillness allowed

Chris to hold her in a romantic gaze, her lovely shape dressed-over by the moonlight – there was just enough glow now to make any man wonder about all that warm beauty she was born with. Poets are supposed to use laughable words in a way that aren't funny – to make them true. Yearning is one of those words – and in the presence of Stephanie and this moonlight, it was the only word that made any sense to him.

Stephanie wasn't thinking about yearning. She was thinking about all the ways she didn't make sense and how hopeless it made her feel. And she resented Chris for pointing out such hopelessness. Yet, it felt good that someone had noticed her paradoxes. Chris seemed to understand her – he just didn't seem to feel her.

"Nietzsche," she said. "Whoever despises still respects themselves as someone who despises. Is that where you're going?"

"Ahh. Aren't fancy educations great? And what have you got?" Chris' body suddenly became lifeless. His adrenaline had left him and he felt as if he was about to collapse. He barely made it back to that overpriced modern chair he hated.

"Stephanie I don't think I know how to obscure my emotions because I usually don't have any. I only can tell you how I am thinking now."

Stephanie walked over to Chris and sat on his lap. She put her arms around his neck and kissed him. "How do you feel then?"

"Doomed."

"Why?"

"Because I am admitting that you chose me because you wanted us to be doomed. Because I am doomed – especially when it comes to you. And that feels like a final verdict somehow – and to be honest, I kinda resent you for making me admit it. But mostly it just scares me, I guess. And really, I mostly fear for you, by the way."

"Chris what the fuck are you talking about?"

"I can't know you. See if you're unknowable you're safe."

"Safe from what!"

"Me or everything, I suppose."

"Chris, you just condemned me to a life of loneliness. Do you even hear the bullshit you're spewing?"

He had no answer for that. Thankfully, his energy returned and he picked Stephanie up and gently placed her on the couch. He didn't look at her as he said, "It usually has a pattern. I meet'em. I can't quite grasp the smart ones. A key piece remains unknowable. So I hurt'em and then I write a poem. I'm like a drunk with my routine."

"Is that what you want to do to me, Chris? Hurt me?"

"No Stephanie – I want to know you. I am just pretty sure you're best left unknown by a guy like me."

Chris' voice suddenly got louder. "You know – some part of you *knows* that I am not the guy for you. I fit your pattern. You fit my pattern. It's just bullshit."

"Screw you Chris! I think you actually care about me but it's safer being a prick. Patterns? What is this *therapy*?"

"I spent 10 grand on shrinks and never got this far to understanding what a prick I am and what denial nutcases my women are."

"You do like me, Chris? Don't you?"

"Say it's true. I like you. I don't know if it is because I don't know what I feel, but if it's true – I like you – than the last thing I'd want is for you to be with me since I know me. I presume you read Catch-22 in college."

"This is such *crap*! You wanna break-up because you care about me?"

"I wanna breakup because I wanna know you." Chris took a deep breath. "I suppose you want to argue about all this for a little while? Hell, let's admit we're romantics: We're argue for a long while...."

He knew Stephanie wanted to argue – not just about their relationship – but to learn something about herself. Chris felt the best their short relationship could be was a learning experience for her. Actually it was an admitting-experience, not learning. She was too smart to not have learned all this a long time ago. But admitting has no IQ – it takes courage and any idiot can have that. In fact, the stupider the better when it comes to courage. It's easy to jump off a cliff if you have no fucking idea about gravity.

Chris picked up a room-temperature wine glass and downed it. Poured another. "I guess it is going to be a long night," he said.

****

Stephanie was dressing now in the bedroom and it was noon outside. Both of them had drank themselves sober and Chris remarked to himself the differences the afternoon inflicts on the beach. Just a few hours ago it had been romantically coy, like an old burlesque stripper. Now it was just cold in its heat and the oncoming waves seemed angry with the blinding sun. The beach was in a rush to get to twilight and beyond. It seemed to hate afternoon as much as Chris did.

Stephanie stood behind him now and without thought, put her arms around his waist. "Chris I wish you'd just take a couple of days and – "

He turned to face her. "Truth is Stephanie you bore –" He couldn't say it. "Truth is, I just don't know Stephanie. But I think if you stop dating Man Buns and fucking guys like me, you might get a powerful mysterious disruption. I hope I was an OK disruption. That'd be a fucking nice thing, believe it or not.

"*Powerful mysterious disruption.* A pretty bad name for a poem, isn't it? I wish I was good enough to turn it around into something. But I know my limits."

"I don't understand you," she whispered. But he could see that didn't really bother her, since she was understanding something about herself now. This impromptu therapy session had provided some insight for her. Perhaps, Chris thought, I have disrupted something in her. Perhaps it won't be as easy to go through the motions with the next guy. Perhaps the next guy won't be the usual next guy. However, he distrusted this, since he felt he wasn't capable of good deeds. Nevertheless, Stephanie's expression was appropriately sad, but her wonderful, smart brown eyes weren't sad – they were alive. And thinking.

"I hope for the best," Chris said – what the fuck did I just say? he thought. He almost told her this whole thing – this *life* between them suddenly felt unjust to him, like she or him were being robbed of a chance for something better. But the more he wanted her, the more he hated who he believed he was – and he was tired, she was tired and it was already a miserable hot afternoon out, and so in seconds, he made sure Stephanie was gone. But then he had that dream....

He sat before a large white clock and watched it tick. It was dream-time, so it felt like he watched it tick for years, but maybe it was only seconds. Nevertheless it ticked on and on and he thought it would never end but suddenly the clock was being filled with water. And he realized as he watched the water rise that the clock had been empty somehow and now the water was making it electric and beautiful and opaque and willing and full – just *full* and everything suddenly started getting twilight-blue around him and then...he woke up.

Chris ran to the bathroom. He could barely breathe. Thoughtlessly, he started a warm bath and immersed himself in it. He never took baths. Despite the fact he lived on the ocean, he never swam in it, but now he was in the water as deep as the tub would let him and only his nose poked above the surface. The warm water felt like pressurized silence on his ears and he thought over and over about calling Stephanie. Just call her. Just call her back here. But he couldn't open his eyes to that thought, so all he saw was that damn clock. He tried to remain still and focused so he could see something else, but nothing else appeared. So he dropped his head completely beneath the water. Maybe it's time to see nothing at all, he thought.

The Hot Black Night

Sitting on this hill now, she is filled with joy watching the sun fall in small steps from the sky. Suddenly, a twinkle of rain here and there land out of the cloudless sky and she feels whole again. It had been a wonderful summer day and soon, it would be a hot black night – but a hot black night with purpose, she thinks. Yes, some jerk had broken her heart yesterday – and sure, her heart is chipped all over because of a past littered with jerks. But choice is something that can change and the breeze now guides a few rain drops onto her lovely brown hair. Her curious blue eyes close and she smiles and thinks about all the ways being young sucks but there is still plenty to love about it, too – the energy and the possibility and the fact that if you play your choices honestly, you might just grow old in kindness. Her baby-white oval face shines off an infectious wonder and she laughs. It is twilight and beautiful here and almost anything can be a laugh in the end, can't it? Because we're all gonna die one day and it's the silliest thing to lie to yourself. And suddenly she sees her whole romantic history synapsed as this: The easiest thing you can do is hurt another human being. There is no grand intelligence or talent to it and in fact – it's the most boring thing to do. The sun falls completely from the sky now leaving a new hot black night ahead full of purpose and possibilities. It's wonderful to not know anything again.

I'm going out tonight to find all sorts of trouble worth a damn, she thinks.

Made in the USA
Lexington, KY
17 April 2017